I0766482

5
Amazing
Fairytales
WRITTEN BY
R. ANDERSON, JR.

ANBORAN
LET OUR MAGIC SURROUND YOU

Table of Contents

The Hairless Bear

Far away, in a remote forest, there lived a bear named Orgis. He was kind and gentle and the most well-mannered of all the creatures in the forest. One evening, as Orgis lay hibernating in his cave, he suddenly grew very cold. He tossed and he turned, trying desperately to get comfortable. But no matter what he tried, he could not keep warm. When the sun rose in the morning, Orgis noticed that all of his fur was on the ground. There was not a single strand of hair on his body. Orgis could not go outside for help, for it was too cold.

An old tiger was passing by the cave that morning when he heard Orgis's howling for help. "Are you alright in there?" asked the tiger.

"No, I'm afraid not," said Orgis, who was in such agony. "What's wrong?" asked the tiger.

"Promise you won't laugh," Orgis said.

"I promise. Now tell me, why all the howling?"

"My fur—it's all gone! And the air is so cold. I'm freezing and cannot get warm!" Orgis confessed.

"Oh, that is bad," said the tiger, moving toward the entrance of the cave. "Where is your family?"

"They're at the other end of the river. Please, my name is Orgis, Will you fetch them for me?"

"Of course!" the tiger said, and off he went to find Orgis's family. Hours later, four bears entered Orgis's cave.
"Orgis, what happened?" his mother asked.

"I don't know," Orgis said. "When I woke up, my fur was just gone. How will I make it through the winter with nothing to keep me warm?"

Orgis's mother snuggled in close to him. Beside her, the others did the same. "Don't worry, Orgis. We will be your fur for however long it takes."

And so, surrounded by the warmth of his family, Orgis settled into a peaceful sleep that carried him through the winter.

At last, spring arrived. Orgis awoke to find his family still lying beside him. After such a long sleep, he was dreadfully hungry, and so he decided to get up to look for food.

Careful not to wake anyone, Orgis snuck out of the cave. But he had no more than set one paw outside when he heard laughter. The squirrels pointed at him, making jokes.

Orgis ignored them and continued to search for food. But each time he came across one of the citizens of the forest, they laughed at him.

"Where is your fur, Orgis?" "Look at the pink bear!" "What an ugly creature!"

Orgis just kept walking, doing his best to pay them no mind.

Meanwhile, on the other side of the forest, a village was being built. Homes were springing up along a deep canal, and a fence had been built that separated the village from the rest of the forest.

One of the village's first residents was an old woman whom everyone called Madea. She was a happy old lady who enjoyed cooking more than anything else.

Each Friday, she would pick one new villager to cook for. And each Friday her guest would join her for a free dinner. Afterward, she would put the leftovers from each dinner into a bowl, and she'd toss them over the fence for the dogs to enjoy.

On one particular Friday, Madea invited her new next-door neighbors over for dinner. They were a young couple, and had a son who was six years old.

Madea had had company for dinner the night before, and had not yet had a chance to toss out the leftovers. When her new guests arrived, she asked the little boy if he could toss yesterday's leftovers over the fence for her. The boy agreed and, taking the bowl, he walked toward the fence.

The boy lifted the bowl up above his head toward the top of the fence. He was about to pour out the leftovers when he heard a voice say, "Wait, little boy! Don't pour those leftovers on the ground. Is that how you treat your friends? How about you bring that down here."

The boy looked around. To his surprise, he found that the fence had a small door. Curious, he lifted the lever that held the door closed. But as soon as he took his first step forward, he slipped and fell into the canal.

As the boy lay there motionless, a pack of vicious wolves came out from amongst the trees.

"Let's eat him now," said one of the wolves.

But the leader of the pack knew that food often came from the old lady. He did not want to eat the boy so close to the old lady's home, and so the wolves grabbed him and started to drag him toward their den, deep in the forest.

When the little boy awoke from his sleep, he did not know where he was. He started to cry.

"Don't cry, little boy, you're in good hands!" said one of the wolves who was following the boy from close behind.

"Where are you taking me?" asked the little boy. "To our home," said the leader of the wolves.

"Why don't you take me back to my home?" asked the little boy.

"Because we're going to eat you," said the leader of the wolves.

The little boy screamed for help as loud as he could. Around him, the wolves began to howl, eager to drown out the boy's voice.

Orgis, who was traveling in this part of the woods heard the wolves howling. "What are they howling at," Orgis thought to himself.
Taking a deep breath, Orgis caught a whiff of a scent that he was not familiar with. He decided to check it out, thinking that perhaps it might be food. As he got closer, he heard the boy crying out for help.

Orgis ran toward the voice. As he neared the wolves, he spied the little boy being dragged away. Orgis knew he had to do something! He quickly took off running toward the wolves, their howls drowning out the sound of his footfalls.

At last, the wolves' leader spoke. "This is close enough. Let's eat him now."

The wolves were just about to pounce on the boy when Orgis appeared from out of nowhere. Standing on a broken tree, he roared at the wolves, and then charged into them.

The wolves fought until Orgis overpowered them.

The wolves retreated, and Orgis told the little boy to climb on his back.

The boy was fearful, but he knew the bear could have let him die. He had chosen to save him. And so he did as he was told.

Orgis traced the wolves' pawprints all the way back to the canal. When they reached the canal, Orgis climbed down and over the fence into Madea's backyard, where he collapsed. He was wounded very badly from his fight with the wolves.

The little boy ran into Madea's home. His parents, who had been out looking for him, were relieved to see him alive. They grabbed him and held him tightly.

Moments later, the little boy's parents ran out the back door to Madea's home. The little boy's mother did not hesitate. She ran over to Orgis, closed her eyes, and placed her hands over his wounds. Slowly, they started to heal. Then Orgis's fur grew back.

Orgis opened his eyes. When he looked upon the little boy's mother, he was shocked.

"Lady Alena, but—you're a fairy! Why are you here—with the humans?"

The boy's mother smiled and nodded. "Yes, Orgis, it is me. Please, do keep my secret."

"I will," said Orgis.

A moment later, the boy's father thanked Orgis for delivering his son from the wolves.

Orgis rose on his feet, bowed his head, and took off into the woods. As he ran, the other animals joined him on his journey back home. They followed him in the trees above and on the ground. They wanted to hear his story.

At home, Orgis's parents ran out to meet him. Beside them stood the old tiger who had helped him find his family.

"Orgis!" yelled the leader of the apes. "We saw how you saved that child's life from those that afflicted him."

"Yeah!" said the leader of the elephants.

"We are sorry for not being there for you when it was you who needed help," said the leader of the lions.

"But should affliction ever befall you again, we promise to be there," said the leader of the apes, and he started to pound on his chest.

And as Orgis held up his paw, all the animals joined in the celebration.

The End

The Candlemaker and the Moon

Once upon a time there lived a candlemaker who dreamed of marrying the moon. The candlemaker lived on a high hill, where he could be closer to his love. At the back of his home was a window, which he called "the Very Large Window." At this window sat a small table with only one chair. It was here the candlemaker would sit, waiting for the moon to rise.

Each night—except those when the moon could not be seen in the sky—the candlemaker laid two sections of the table with food. The end that faced toward the window was for him, and the end opposite him was for his date, the moon.

And each night, the moon passed by the window, rising from the bottom up, until it had passed out of sight. When the moon was stationed directly in the middle of the window, he greeted her, saying, "Hello, beloved, it's quite the honor to have you join me for dinner tonight."

As long as the moon remained before the window, the candlemaker would remain at the table. He talked about his day, and about the weird customers that stopped by his booth at the market where he worked. And just before the moon rose above the window where it could no longer be seen, the candlemaker would make his daily wish for the moon to be his, and his alone.

One evening, the candlemaker was preparing dinner as usual when a little man, who just so happened to be passing by, smelled the sweet aroma of the food he was cooking. The man walked over to the candlemaker's door and gave it a few knocks. When the candlemaker opened the door, the man asked for a plate of food.

"I'm sorry," said the candlemaker. "I only have enough food for two, and I have a very special guest stopping by tonight."

The little man studied the candlemaker. At last he said, "If you give me the extra portion, I'll grant you just one of your heart's desires."

The candlemaker scratched his head, thinking about the little man's words.

"If you can grant me my desires," said the candlemaker, "Then why don't you bring forth your own food?"

"I don't know how to cook," said the little man, "And besides, I have never smelled anything so delightful as the aromas coming from your kitchen."

The candlemaker shook his head. "I don't think you can give me what I want."

"Oh please, just ask me. Please, anything. I simply must have whatever it is you're cooking in there."

The candlemaker quickly blabbered out his heart's true desire. "I want the moon, and I don't want to have to share it."

"The moon will be yours," the little man said, and he threw his hands up in the air. "Yes, it will! It will be—tonight. Now please, fetch me some of that food you're cooking in there."

The candlemaker invited the little man in, and he gave him the one seat at his table, as well as his own portion of the food. When the little man was done eating, he grabbed his things to go, but the candlemaker quickly stopped him.

"Where is my moon?" asked the candlemaker.

"Don't worry," said the little man, "The moon shall be yours tonight, just as I said. Goodbye."

And with that, the little man departed.

That night, the candlemaker sat at his table, as he did each night. He waited for the moon to arrive at his window, but the moon did not show up. After hours of waiting, the candlemaker grew frustrated. He hopped up from the table, grabbed his coat, and went out looking for the moon. When he got outside, he found a beautiful young woman sitting at the edge of the cliff, staring up into the sky.

Curious, the candlemaker asked her name.

The young woman replied that she did not have a name. As far as she could remember, she had always been called the Moon.

The candlemaker asked her what she was doing outside his home, and she told him that she had fallen from the sky.

At this, the candlemaker grew quite excited, for he knew why she was there, even if she did not know herself. He put his coat around her and told her that she could live with him. Then, showing her inside, he brought her to her seat at his table and gave her dinner.

After she ate, the candlemaker led the young woman to one of the rooms in his home. "This is your room," he said. "Do with it as you please. The bed is very comfortable. I'm sure you'll like it. I had it custom built for you, and there are also clothes for you in the closet."

"Thank you," said the Moon.

The candlemaker closed her door and went over to his room. That night, he dreamed of marrying the moon. The next day, the candlemaker jumped out of bed and hurried over to the room prepared for the moon. He wanted to see if there was someone there.

When he opened the door, he saw the woman sitting on the bed.

It was not a dream! the candlemaker thought. "Did you sleep well?" he asked her.
"I have not had any sleep," said the Moon.

The Moon explained that she did not know how to fall asleep, and that whatever sleep was, she had never experienced it before.

The candlemaker couldn't believe what he was hearing. He told the moon that he needed to go to work, but that he would be back before sunset.

"Stay here," he said. "When I get home, I will make you a big dinner."

The Moon nodded, telling him that she had no place to go. Then she lay down on the bed and closed her eyes.

At the market, everyone was talking about the strange darkness that had come over the earth during the night, and how they had never seen such darkness before. Delighted as he was by the moon's company, the candle-maker had not noticed how dark it was.

As the candlemaker sat there waiting for someone to buy candles from him, he noticed that it had begun to get dark earlier than usual.

The gardener, who had the booth across from his, noticed it as well. Walking over to the candlemaker, he said, "Something is not right. The sun has only been up for a few hours, and look, the night is already upon us."

"Indeed," said the candlemaker.

Telling the gardener that he needed to get home right away, the candlemaker closed his booth and hurried home as fast as he could. When he got there, he heard the Moon singing.

Seeing the candlemaker, she took him by the hand and the two danced together in the field of grass.

"I was going to prepare a big dinner for you tonight," said the candlemaker. "But the sun soared across the sky in a matter of hours, and the night came earlier than usual."

The Moon smiled and said to him, "The sun searches for me." "Well, he can't have you," said the candlemaker in a serious tone.

"You're right. I cannot go back. Not unless you release me," said the Moon. "As long as I'm here, people will suffer."

"That's fine with me," said the candlemaker. "I'm not suffering. I have you here with me."

"Take your eyes off of me for a moment," the Moon said. "Look up into the sky. Tell me, what do you see?"

The candlemaker looked up into the sky. "I see stars. They appear to be moving for some odd reason."

"The earth is spinning much faster than normal," said the Moon.

"Why are you telling me all of this?" the candlemaker asked. "You belong here with me, forever. I will never let you go."

"That must be a human thing. To be selfish," said the Moon.

"Well, I don't think so," said the candlemaker. "I'm happy . . . more so than ever before!" he shouted.

"But I'm not," said the Moon.

At the Moon's words, the candlemaker became angry. He took off into the woods alone, not realizing how dark it was until he got far away from his home. He was so upset at the moon that he kept walking into the dark woods, where there was barely any light.

"I heard your conversation," said a leopard that was resting in the top of a tree. "You're pretty brave walking out here alone."

The candlemaker ignored the leopard and kept on walking. The leopard hopped down from the tree and started to follow behind the candlemaker. "You're the one responsible for there being no moon tonight."

The candlemaker realized that the leopard was following him, so he sped up his pace. "Put the moon back," the leopard growled.

Just ahead of him, the candlemaker heard laughter and people talking. He started to run.

Breaking out of the woods, he found a crowd gathered around a huge bonfire.

The candlemaker turned and looked back, but the leopard was gone.
"Are you okay?" asked one of the men who was standing around the fire.

"Yes, there was a leopard chasing me," said the candlemaker, who stood trying to catch his breath.

"Come sit down," said the man. "He's probably long gone by now. We've built this nice bonfire to keep us warm. The people you see here are all poor. We can't afford to buy new candles like the rich, and we used the ones we had last night to see through the strange darkness that came upon us all. Come now, sit down and enjoy the heat with us."

The candlemaker had just settled in and was enjoying the people's company and stories when someone screamed. A young woman and her daughter staggered out of the woods. They had been on their way to the bonfire when they had been mugged.

The people who were gathered around the bonfire followed the young woman to the scene of the crime. There, they saw the little girl's father on the ground. He had been beaten badly by muggers.

The candlemaker stood there looking, but said nothing. He knew this was his doing, for he had removed the light from the world.

"Look, the sun is starting to rise," said one of the onlookers. "Already?" asked an old woman.

The candlemaker remembered that he had not made any sales the day before, so he caught the first ride out to the market. When he arrived, he saw many people upset because they were not being allowed into the market; it had been shut off by order of the king.

A lady who knew the candlemaker ran up to him and said, "The market has been ransacked by looters."

The candlemaker hopped down from the carriage and ran over to his booth. When he got there, he found it in shambles. Every last one of his candles was gone.

The candlemaker started to pick up around his booth, but before he knew it, the sun started to set again.

Closing up, he quickly headed home.

As he traveled down the road, the candlemaker came to the village of Samzu— a village for the poor. He always passed through Samzu on his way home, though he usually took little note of it.

On this night, though, he saw that all the windows had candles in them. Walking up to one of the windows, he grabbed one of the candles. Upon the candle was his name. He knew then that it was either the poor who had ransacked his booth or that someone had robbed him and given all of his candles to them.

The candlemaker placed the candle he had taken from the window into his pocket and continued on his way toward the woods that separated him from his home. The candlemaker had always passed through the woods with no problems, but this time he found that he was afraid to walk into the woods because of the leopard that had chased him the night before.

The sun was now down, and it was darker than normal. The candlemaker lit the candle he had taken from the window to light his way through the woods.

Slowly, he stepped into the woods. The candlemaker knew he could not run, lest the light from the candle should blow out. Still, he was eager to be out of the woods and back home, where the moon was waiting for him.

As he was walking through the woods, the candlemaker heard a voice say, "I heard your conversation."

The candlemaker recognized the voice. It was the leopard. He turned to look for him, using the light from the candle, but he could not spot the leopard because it was too dark.

"You're pretty brave walking out here alone," the leopard said.

"What do you want from me?" yelled the candlemaker into the darkness. Out of nowhere, the leopard pounced upon him and knocked him down.

The candlemaker pushed the leopard's paws off of him and took off running through the woods until he reached the field that led up to his home. When he made it through the field, he saw the Moon. She was standing there, by the edge of the cliff, staring into the sky.

"Moon," said the candlemaker. "I've been selfish. I've been very selfish.
I just wanted to have you all to myself. And I wanted you to love me alone,
like I love you."

"I know," said the Moon. "But I can't love you alone because you're not the
only one that loves me. There's no number to the forms of life that love me
and depend on me each and every day. Even the leopard that seeks your
life loves me," said the Moon as she continued to gaze into the sky.

"You're right," the candlemaker admitted. "Some things belong to
everyone, and they're better off not being in the hands of only one person.
It is those things I now know are meant to be enjoyed by everyone." The
candlemaker touched the Moon's hand. "I'm going to miss you, but you're
right, you belong in the sky above—I release you."

The Moon turned to face the candlemaker. Smiling, she said, "Tomorrow
evening, same time?"

"Yes," said the candlemaker with a big smile on his face. "I'll prepare dinner. too."

The Moon stepped back, and then she vanished into thin air.

The candlemaker stood there for a few seconds. Then he turned and started to walk toward his home.

From the forest's edge, he heard a voice. "Thank you."

The candlemaker turned and faced the leopard. As they stood there, the moon rose above the two of them.

With a last look up, the leopard turned and disappeared into the woods.

The next day, when the candlemaker returned to the market, his booth had been repaired, and all the stolen candles had been returned.

The End

Changing Beautiful

Long ago, in the days of old, before men distanced themselves from magic, there lived a young princess named Beautiful.

Beautiful's mother adored her, and her father—the king of Chanea—spent much of his time bestowing his wealth upon the girl, for it seemed but a small thing to him to beautify his heir.

In those days, it was very uncommon for a king to love his daughter so openly. Usually it was the sons whom the kings preferred and praised in public. But Beautiful's father was different; he never hid his love for his daughter.

In fact, so deep was the king's love that he declared Beautiful's Eve a national holiday. And on Beautiful's Eve, the fathers could bring their daughters to the castle to dance with them before the King. The highlight of the night was always the King and his daughter, who were the last to dance.

The king's love for Beautiful was quite contagious. Beautiful grew and was beloved by the people of Chanea, especially the men, who wished to follow in the king's footsteps.

Beautiful was a fine young lady, but there was one thing missing. She had never been taught Life's Gift. Her parents felt she could do no wrong, so they rarely corrected her. And although Beautiful was blessed with beauty, she hardly gave it any thought. She overlooked the poor and had little pity on the animals that she came in contact with.

The people of Chanea began talking amongst themselves. It was quite obvious to them that the King and Queen had failed to teach Beautiful about Life's Gift, but no one dared to question them.

One day, visitors arrived from a foreign land. The King ordered his mimes to put on their best performance for his guests at dinner. One of the performers, a man named Puck, reached into his pocket and pulled out a slingshot. He loaded it with a pebble, pulled back, aimed, and released. Within seconds, the small pebble struck the other mime on the behind.

"Ouch!" he shouted, and everyone at the table burst into laughter.

Beautiful felt she had witnessed the most amazing thing ever. She had never seen people laughing so hard. She leaned over to her father and asked, "Father, what's that thingamajig called?"

"It's called a slingshot," said the King.

"Can I have one?" asked Beautiful, "I want to make people laugh, too."

The King called Puck over. "Puck, Beautiful would like one of those slingshots. Tell me, where can we get her one?"

"She can have this one," said Puck. "I have another."

Over the next few months, Beautiful used her new slingshot to sting everyone she came in contact with. She spared no one, not even the King and Queen. She thought it was just harmless fun, but Olivia and Lucenda, the witches who worked in the castle, soon grew tired of being stung by the slingshot.

"We have to do something," said Olivia.

"I know," said Lucenda, "but what?"

"What about the elder trees?" asked Olivia.

"A great idea!" said Lucenda. "Yes, we will go to them!"

Later that night, Olivia and Lucenda met with the elder trees of the forest. They told them of the pains that they all had to endure in the home of the King on account of Beautiful, the King's daughter.

"We will take your message to the Great Spring," said the trees. "He will know what to do."

In those days, certain rainbow trees could walk and talk, but they did it only on rare occasions. "Thank you," said Olivia. "We need to get back to the castle before someone comes looking for us."

Meanwhile, deep in the forest, the elder trees sought the Great Spring. They came to a cave that contained a beautiful blue spring. The eldest tree of the elder trees stepped forward and spoke into the cave, "Oh, Great Spring who gives life to life, hear the Great Trees who give life to life."

Suddenly, a voice from within the cave commanded, "Speak."

The eldest tree of the elder trees spoke into the cave all the things that the two witches had told them of Beautiful. When. He was done speaking, he and the rest of the rainbow trees departed into the forest.

The next day, Beautiful went out to the royal pond for a swim. She took off her gown and stepped into the water. But when she got about waist deep, the water began to vibrate. "What kind of magic is this?" she asked.

A voice said, "A life for a life." "Who's there?" asked Beautiful.

The water started to vibrate again. "That which is seen shall be seen no more until Beautiful beholds what life bestows."

Immediately, the water started to glow.

Beautiful tried to get out of the water, but her legs vanished right before her eyes. "What is this?" she asked. With one last breath, she screamed very loudly before her entire body was consumed by the nothingness.

Everyone in the castle came running outside to the royal pond, but they were too late.

"Where is Beautiful?" yelled the King angrily. "Where is my daughter?"

Beautiful tried to get her father's attention, but no one there could see her or hear her.

"Search the area! Find my daughter," the King shouted.

Months passed, but still there was no sign of the princess. At last, the King's royal advisors told him the time had come to call off the search. The King did not want to give up, but his advisors told him that the men were exhausted. They were ready to come home to be with their families. "What about my family?" the king asked. Angry, he locked himself in his room and hid from his duties as King. All he wanted was to see his daughter again, and in good health.

Beautiful watched her father from afar, devastated. For months she had stood, unseen, forced to watch her parents suffer. But now, this was too much. To see her father lock himself up and refuse to eat was more than she could bear. And so, whispering a goodbye, she left the castle.

Soon, Beautiful came to a nearby village. She had visited it as a little girl, but not again since then. Beautiful decided to look around. Perhaps someone here can help me, she thought.

Beautiful approached the closest house. Inside she saw a single chair. Everything else had been removed.

Confused, Beautiful spent many hours going from one home to another, but each one was equally empty.

On the third day of her search, she came across an old man named Eso, who was fending off a gang of bullies trying to steal from an old woman. The bullies proved to be no match for him. They took off running after old Eso struck them a few times with his cane.

Eso helped the old woman up and sent her on her way. Curious, Beautiful decided to follow old Eso.

Days passed, and still Beautiful followed the man. She watched all of his dealings, and learned that he was a kindhearted old man from whom she could learn much. Eso did not have much, but he gave a lot. He grew a garden in his backyard to feed the poor of the village, and he did not require them to help him in keeping up the garden. He visited the orphans, and he cooked meals for the blind lady who lived next door to him.

Early one morning, Eso rushed out of his bed. Grabbing his things, he stormed out of the house.

Beautiful took off behind him. What could be wrong? she wondered.

That morning, Eso did not follow his normal routine. Instead, she noticed Eso walked and walked until he reached the next village over.

As they neared the village, Beautiful saw a giant blue wolf. She tried to warn Eso to stop and to turn around, but he could not hear her.

"Stay where you are," said the wolf.
Beautiful stood there, terrified, but Eso kept walking until he reached the village.

"Come closer," said the giant wolf. "I will not hurt you." Beautiful took a few steps forward.
"I am Odu."

"You can see me, Odu?" asked Beautiful.

"Anyone who has a pure heart can see you, Beautiful. What brings you here?"

"I was following Eso," said Beautiful.

"Have you heard the news of your father?" asked Odu.

"I'm afraid not. Is he okay?" asked Beautiful, a look of concern on her face. "He is dying," said Odu.
"No!" said Beautiful. She turned to run back to Chanea, but Odu moved in front of her.

"No one can help you there. There is a boy here in the village. He wears a blue scarf, and he's standing on the overpass. He can help you."

Beautiful took off toward the village. On the overpass, she saw a lot of people going back and forth.

What do I do?

Then it came to her. She screamed as loud as she could, but the people continued to pass her by, not noticing her at all.

At that moment, a young man ran up to her, "Hey there. Are you alright?"

Beautiful noticed the blue scarf the boy was wearing.

"I'm Doyin. Are you alright?" he asked again.
"I was trying to get your attention," Beautiful said, staring into his eyes.
"Well, here I am. What's your name?" he asked.
"Beautiful," she replied.

He paused, as if he had just heard the greatest news ever. "The Beautiful?" asked Doyin. "The princess who went missing months ago?"

"Yes," Beautiful replied, putting her head down in shame.

"This is big. Your father! We have to get you to him right away! Come on. Everyone in the world has been looking for you," said Doyin. He reached for Beautiful's hand, but his own hand passed right through hers.

Beautiful took two steps backward. "I can explain," said Beautiful.
"What just happened?" asked Doyin.
"Do you believe in magic?" asked Beautiful.

"Of course," said Doyin.

"Then you'll believe me when I say magic is what happened to me."
Beautiful hunched her shoulders and started to tell Doyin her story.

"I have an idea," Doyin said when he heard Beautiful's story. "Follow me."
Beautiful followed Doyin to the entrance of the village, where she had
talked with Odu.

"Can you give us a lift?" Doyin asked the wolf. "I can. Climb aboard," said
Odu.
"You two know each other?" asked Beautiful as she and Doyin both
climbed onto Odu's back.

"Yes," said Doyin.

Beautiful looked to him for more information, but he said nothing more.

"Alright now, hold on tight," said Odu. "We're going invisible."

Odu took off toward Chanea. When they had made it to the royal road that led up to the castle, Odu slowed down. A long line of people filled the road to the castle.

"What's going on here?" said Doyin.

"It's Beautiful's Eve in Chanea," said Beautiful.

"Beautiful's Eve, huh? You have your own holiday?" asked Doyin with a look of wonder.

"It's just named after me," said Beautiful.

"I'd love to have a holiday named after me. That's grand," said Doyin with excitement.

"I hope we're not too late," said Beautiful.

"Don't worry, you'll see your father soon," said Doyin.

One of the guards standing at the gate shouted, "The legend is true—look!" Odu was no longer invisible.

The crowd turned and saw the giant blue wolf charging toward them. The people were terrified and started to flee.

"Close the gates, close the gates!" the guards all shouted. But Odu just leaped over the castle gate.
Meanwhile, inside the castle, Beautiful's mother had somehow managed to get the King to attend Beautiful's Eve. He sat in the seat prepared for him, but he didn't look well.

Suddenly, Odu broke through the giant glass window and landed in the middle of the floor. The crowd marveled at the site.

"It's the blue wolf!" some of the people shouted from the crowd.

The King sat there without a care. He was too heartbroken to pay them any mind.

As the guards stormed the room, Doyin hopped down from Odu's back. "Everyone, listen. I've found the princess. She's right here."

The King opened his eyes, and the Queen stood up. The guards grabbed Doyin by his clothes.

"Wait! Just wait a minute!" said Doyin. "Let me explain. She's really right here!" he shouted. But no one would listen to him.

"I'm telling you all, she's right there!" Doyin kept repeating.

The crowd started to laugh and make fun of Doyin. No one could see Beautiful.

Odu could no longer take their insults. He took a very deep breath, which startled the crowd that surrounded him. Then he let out a howl so long and so loud that the room lit up very bright, and the people had to cover their ears.

Suddenly, Odu's appearance changed from blue to gold. A shimmer filled the room, and everyone could see Beautiful standing there.

"It's the princess!" they shouted.

The people in the room were stunned.

Odu's howl faded, and Beautiful faded from view.

The King dropped his arm and fell dead in his chair instantly.

Doyin turned to Beautiful. "Sometimes we have to give up the most precious things we possess in this world in order to protect life. Only life can beget life."

"What are you saying?" asked Beautiful.

"Life's Lesson," said Doyin. "You don't know Life's Lesson?" Beautiful shook her head.
"Some things can't be explained with words; you have to experience them yourself," said Doyin. He moved his left hand close to Beautiful's cheek as though there was no barrier between his hand and her intangible flesh. The crowd watched Doyin as he stood there talking to Beautiful. Unable to see her, it seemed that Doyin was talking to a ghost.

"May your curse fall upon me, Beautiful," Doyin said. "And may my portion here in the land of the living be with you."

"Doyin, no!" said Beautiful. "This is my—" But before she could finish her sentence, Doyin vanished before her eyes.

The crowd was bewildered. "Curse," said Beautiful.
And with that, Beautiful became visible again. Tears rolled down her eyes.

Just then, she remembered her father. Beautiful did not know that her father had fallen over dead in his chair. She only knew that she needed to get to him right away. She had to let him know that she was alive.

Beautiful turned toward her father and ran up the steps to where he was seated on his throne.

"Get up, Father, get up, you have to live, you have to live!" said Beautiful. But the king was dead. "Father, no! Father, no! Please! I'm here, it's me, your daughter!" Beautiful yelled at his lifeless body.

"The King is dead?" asked one of the spectators. The Queen was afraid to look upon her husband.

Beautiful got up and ran over to the giant gold horn above her father's throne. "Beautiful, what are you doing?" asked her mother.
Beautiful stared at her father before blowing as hard as she could into the giant gold horn, which let out a blast so loud that her father woke up from his sleep.

Beautiful ran over to him and embraced him. "You're alive, my father is alive!" she shouted with joy.

"Beautiful, is that you?" asked her father. "Yes, it's me, Father, I'm here." Her father hugged her tightly.

Beautiful was glad that her father was alive, but, she realized, Doyin had sacrificed himself for her.

She turned and stared at the empty space where he last stood. She could not see him, but she knew he was there. Her heart was not as pure as Doyin's heart, but it was starting to become pure.

"Let's go, Odu," said Doyin. "Let's go home."

Odu and Doyin turned and started walking toward the exit. Beautiful saw Odu heading towards the exit, and that's when Doyin's words came to her.

"I understand," Beautiful said to herself. "I understand, Father!" she said out loud. "All life comes from life. Oh, Father, I wish I could stay." Beautiful wiggled herself out of her father's arms. "I have to fix this," she said. "Where are you going?" asked her father.
"I love you, okay? And I'll be watching you, the both of you," Beautiful told her parents.

Beautiful ran down the steps to catch Odu before he left the room.

"Odu! Wait!" Beautiful shouted across the room.

Odu paused, but Doyin kept on walking toward the exit. Odu turned and looked back toward Beautiful.

"Oh, Odu, I understand now. Life is the gift, and life must protect life. I just watched someone who I hardly even know give up his life for me. And I cannot say that I'm so deserving of such a sacrifice. But I know, Odu, that I cannot let Doyin do this. I was the one who needed a lesson from life. And I learned from life that I must protect life."

Odu stared into Beautiful's eyes.

"I'm ready, Odu," said Beautiful. "I'm ready to go wherever the universe is willing to take me. Make me invisible again." Beautiful closed her eyes and said to herself, "Only life can bestow life."

Odu nodded his head as a sign of approval. He gathered his breath and howled as he had before. The room lit up and shined like a polished gold bar. Beautiful opened her eyes and saw Doyin walking toward the exit.

"Doyin!" Beautiful shouted.

Doyin stopped and turned to face Beautiful.

"This is my burden!" said Beautiful. "It is mine alone to bear. May the curse which you took upon yourself rest upon me, and may you enjoy what life bestows—life."

At that, the curse broke. Both Doyin and Beautiful were free. They ran and hugged each other.

The crowd burst into cheers.

Outside, it started to thunder, and then rain started to fall. A gust of wind blew open the huge double doors that led to the back of the castle. Odu looked at Doyin. "You're going to make a fine king," he said.

And with that, Odu walked out into the rain and disappeared. Some say he was the Great Spring. I say he was life itself.

The King stood up and lifted his hand to silence the crowd. And when they all had quieted down, he turned to Doyin and said, "Life must protect life. And here you are, reminding us of why our fathers kept this tradition so sacred."

The King walked down to the middle of the floor where Beautiful and Doyin stood. "I remember my father teaching me those words, although I have not followed in his footsteps so well."

The King turned towards his people and lifted up his voice.

"It is not always wise to wait to do right," said the King as he turned back to face Doyin.

"Doyin," said the King, "I offer you a place here with us in Chanea. A man who can sacrifice himself for the good of another, and who understands that all life must protect life, is fit to rule a kingdom someday."

The King paused and smiled. "Thank you—thank you for bringing our Beautiful back to us."

The King kneeled then, and so did everyone in his presence.

Later on that year, Doyin and Beautiful were engaged, and a legend was born.

The End

Restoring Joy

Long ago, in an era before this one, the world was ruled by three kings: the King of Orman, the King of Roshire, and the King of Barseth. The empire of Boshire was the greatest of them all, but the empire of Barseth was not too far behind the others in glory.

One evening, in the cold of winter, in the north of Roshire, all three kings met around a large table known as the Great Onyx Table in the Field of Kings to discuss border arrangements and what should be done with the new territories that were being divided up amongst them. After they came to an agreement, the King of Roshire spoke, saying, "Brothers, it is done. We have settled the issues here. Let us go now from this place and enjoy what is ours for a thousand generations to come."

But the King of Orman was not so pleased with the agreements. He wanted to rule over a vast empire like Roshire and Barseth, but there was no more land to be divided amongst them. The Great Race for Glory was over, and the King of Roshire would be honored as the winner, for it had been agreed upon long ago by their fathers before them that whoever's empire expanded the most would be recognized as the greatest empire in the world.

The words of the King of Barseth appeared to be well-received by all three kings, but just when they were about to depart from the table, a woman appeared in their midst wearing a velvet cloak. She kept her head down so that no one could see her face.

"Who are you?" asked the King of Roshire.

A voice spoke, saying, "Otepaa," but no one knew from whence the voice came. Otepaa started to walk toward the Great Onyx Table, but the king's bodyguards stood in her way with their weapons drawn.

"Let her come near," said the King of Orman. And the bodyguards did as the King said and escorted her to the table.

"What brings you here?" asked the King of Roshire. Otepaa lifted up her head, but she did not open her mouth.

A voice came again a second time. "My Lords have not conquered all, for there yet remains land. To him that conquers the land I shall disclose, let him be ruler of all."

The kings stared at each other, confused. They could not believe that there remained land that had not been conquered. "What's in it for you, for bringing us this information?" said the King of Barseth.

A voice echoed, "I am an enchantress. I will reveal the land, for asylum in your lands," said Otepaa.

"Where is this land?" asked the King of Orman.

"I will tell thee, only if thou grant me the asylum I seek."

The three kings saw Otepaa's offer an opportunity to gain more glory and gold, and so they agreed to give her asylum.

"Are we able to take the lands?" asked the King of Roshire. "Yes, but I suggest you use my magic," said Otepaa.

"What enchantment will you perform for us?" said the King of Barseth.

The voice spoke again. "Take their joy, and you'll remove the people's peace. If this is thy desire, thou shall surely reap."

The kings all agreed it was their desire, and Otepaa removed four pouches from her side—one brown and the other three yellow. She set a yellow pouch before each of the three kings. Then, untying the brown pouch, she poured a substance onto the center of the Great Onyx Table.

Taking a torch, Oteppa threw its flame onto the substance. A large blue flame went up into the air.

The voice spoke again. "The land thou seeks and its people are one. Ebres it is and Ebres thou shall see. To see thy desires, cast thy pouch before thee into the open flame."

One by one, each king threw his pouch into the open flame. When the last king cast his pouch in the flame, a flash of light so bright that no one could look upon it spread forth from the flame. After the flash passed away, they saw a young boy and a young girl—twins—lying in the middle of the table. The kings were stunned, as were their guests.

The enchantress took off her cloak and cast it over the children.

"Who are these children?" asked the king of Barseth.

"Behold the joy of the people whom you are soon to conquer," said Ote-paa. She told them that the joy of the people had taken on human form. She then gave each of the kings an emerald key, and to one of the body-guards standing nearby, she gave a chain with a lock attached to it. The lock required all three emerald keys in order to be opened.

Oteppa instructed the guards to place the chain around the wrists of both the boy and the girl, and to hold them both as prisoners.

"We don't need their joy. We can defeat them without this sort of magic," said the King of Barseth. "Together, we are unbeatable."

"Not if you want to win the battle. You have to take everything from these people: their history, culture, and everything that connects them with this land. If not, the land will give them the victory over you," said Otepaa.

The kings all agreed to follow her advice. They each went their way, and joy was held as a prisoner in Roshire.

A year later, ships from all three empires arrived off the coast of Ebres. A member of the O'toki tribe spotted the ships and brought word back to the elders of Ebres. The elders, along with many of their men and women, went out to meet the strangers.

At first, everything seemed to be well. They exchanged gifts with the strangers, and then one of the members of the O'toki tribe spotted a woman walking on the water toward them. It was Otepaa.

She came ashore and stood before the chief of the O'toki tribe. She reached out her hand and touched the chief in the center of his head. Within seconds, the O'toki people started to hallucinate. They started to see the strangers in a different light. They no longer looked like people from Roshire, Orman, or Barseth. Their attire changed, and they appeared as gods in the flesh. Otepaa ordered the men to take them as servants.

From the east to the west, Otepaa stood by the army until they conquered all of Ebres. There was not one tribe that could stand before the armies of the three kings. For Otepaa had removed the heart of the people and cast it into an ocean of oblivion.

The empire of Roshire proved strongest, and over time, all of Ebres fell under their control. They forced their newfound servants to build them fine palaces and elaborate cities to enjoy for themselves and their children for a hundred generations to come.

In time, a descendant of the King of Roshire relocated to Ebres, and there he was set up as king over the entire country. After much gain and many years of

dispute, the new King of Ebres decreed that the people of Ebres should be granted their freedom, but he was too late; the window of opportunity had closed for him to do well by the people.

In the fourth year of the king's reign, a strange thing began to take place in Ebres. The people of Ebres started to change into what the people called brutes. Brutes were humans, but changed. A great rage overcame them, and they took on the form of ferocious beasts. These beasts had the power to turn anyone into one of them. They were beyond saving.

While the people of Ebres were changing into brutes, the remaining people of Ebres tried to flee. Those who had not changed did not want to become like the   beasts.

Word eventually reached the sons of the three kings, who were now ruling over the old empires. They had gathered for a meeting in Roshire to discuss the situation in Ebres. Their people were demanding that they do something about the brutes, fearful of what they were hearing from their loved ones in Ebres.

The kings called for their astrologers and their priests, but both were of no help. As each day passed by, more and more people changed into brutes, sometimes an entire village in a day.

The enchantress who had long ago appeared before their fathers had passed away, and without her the kings were at a loss. They sought counsel from their oracles, who all referred them to an old hag, the best in her time. She told the kings that their fathers were cruel to the people of Ebres, and that if they wanted to return to the days of peace and prosperity, they would need to restore joy to the people.

The kings agreed to break their treaty, which had been in effect for many years. They set out to meet the twins, whom their fathers had imprisoned in a castle built in the mountains of Roshire.

When they reached the old castle, they found Joy still living in human form. There was not the slightest wrinkle on them, for they had not aged one bit. When they opened the chamber doors to where Joy was, Joy asked them why they had come. The King of Barseth stepped forward and told them that all three kings had agreed to release them from their bondage.

"Go, save your people," said the King of Barseth. And each king placed the emerald key that was passed down to them by their fathers into the special lock made by Otepaa. When the chains fell to the ground, Joy smiled at the kings before vanishing before their eyes.

Back in Ebres, the descendants of the people of Roshire, Orman, and Barseth were ordered to flee to the Black Mountain. There, the King of Ebres had gathered his men inside of a large fort at the top of the mountain. They knew the people of Ebres treated the Black Mountain as sacred grounds, and they were right. The brutes surrounded the base of the mountain, but they did not attempt to climb it.

On the far side of the mountain, a little boy climbed, trying to get away from the brutes. His mother and father had been among the first to change, but their son's life had been spared.

The little boy reached for a hole in the side of the mountain, but his hand slipped, and he started to fall toward the ground. The brutes on the ground below watched in delight as the boy fell toward the ground.

But before he reached the base of the mountain, a hand scooped him up—a brute who had followed him. The little boy opened his eyes to find his father was standing over him in human form.

"Let's go, son. We need to make it to the fort," said the boy's father as he helped him up.

Together, the two reached the top of the mountain, but the people did not want to let the boy's father in. One of the guards who stood watch had seen the boy's father change from a brute back to a human.

"He's been infected by the plague," said the guard.

The boy's father begged them to let him in, but the people refused. They sent out two of their guards to retrieve the boy, but they were unsuccessful. The boy's father was a very strong man, and he was not so easy to take down.

The people sent out two more guards. They forced the father and boy apart, and with their spears, they pushed the father to the edge of the cliff. The little boy screamed so loudly that the brutes who were watching down below heard his cry. The brutes charged up the mountain to save the little boy and his father. When they were halfway up, Joy appeared before them.

Joy smiled, then took off running toward the brutes. As Joy and the brutes collided, a burst of light and wind exploded. The wind traveled down the mountain, into the field, and through the woods.

Standing firm, Joy reminded the brutes of who they were and where they had come from.

The people in the fort watched in terror as the wind from the clash shook the fort violently. To the guards' surprise, the brutes changed back into humans.

At once, the mountain was covered with the people of Ebres—among them men, women, and children who were Roshirans, Ormans, and Barsethians by descent.

They stood together, watching as the doors to the fort opened and the King, along with a small infantry, stepped out.

The King of Ebres approached the elders of Ebres.

"I do not know where to start the process of healing for your people and my people," he began. "But on behalf of my people, we choose to start with an apology to your people for our offenses and the offenses of our fathers toward your people. Our ancestors failed to see what nature continues to try and teach—that no man can prevent the sun from setting upon him or his kingdom.

No matter how great he is, the darkness will come, and the moon will rise. But that doesn't mean that that man or his people have to be afraid of the night, because if he learns that he cannot prevent the sun from setting, then he ought to know that he cannot prevent the sun from rising either. The light will come and the darkness shall leave."

The King had a table prepared before him and the people of Ebres on the mountain. He invited the elders of the tribes to sit at his table, and there they discussed new laws and issues that have been held between their people since the days of old.

And that was the beginning of a new world.

The End

Everla and the Stone Prince

There once lived a young prince named Sakima who dreamt of being great and powerful. One day he snuck into the chamber of wonders—a secret room located within his castle. There he found the writings of Hinun, the teacher of Koda, who had become the most powerful wizard of all time. After reading the writings of Hinun, the young prince decided that he, too, wanted to become a wizard. But to do so, he needed Koda's wand. The young prince thought that having the wand would make him great. He thought that his people would both love him and fear him at the same time, like they had Koda in the writings of Hinun. And, as chance would have it, he knew exactly where it was—and how to get it.

Each year, Sakima was granted a single birthday with from his father—anything he wanted. This year, for his thirteenth birthday, he decided to ask for the most powerful treasure that was within his father's possession: the Wand of Hinun.

At last, the sun rose on the prince's thirteenth birthday. He ran to find his parents—to tell his father of his birthday wish. But as soon as he opened his door, he walked into a surprise celebration.

His family and his friends were all there, gathered together to see him. Among the guests was his uncle, who handed him his gift.

"This belonged to an old friend of mine who is no longer with us. I figured you would appreciate having this in your collection."

The young prince opened the gift. It was a diary! Curious, Sakima excused himself to read the book. To his surprise, it had belonged to a wizard who had recently died. The prince walked out onto his balcony, which over-looked the Sea of Hinun. There he sat, reading the words of the old wizard.

While Sakima was sitting there, his father burst in on him.

"Son, what is this thing that thou desires the most, since today is thy born date? Ask anything, and it shall be granted," said the King.

The prince politely closed his book and said, "Father, I desire the wand of Hinun."

At this, the King became sad. He was excited that his son was now thirteen, and was proud of the young man he was turning out to be. And yet, the boy's request grieved him to his heart. He had promised to give the prince whatever he desired, but he did not know that the young prince knew about the wand of Hinun.

Seconds later, the young prince's mother walked onto the balcony. "So what did our beloved prince ask for?"
"He asked for the wand of Hinun," said the King in a muffled voice.

The Queen turned and stared at the King in dismay. "Well, he can't have it," she said.

Sakima jumped up. "But Mother, Father promised!"

The King and Queen both knew that something so powerful as the wand should not be placed in the hands of a child, but the King wanted to honor his word.

"Come with me," the King said, and he led his son to the wing of the castle where the chamber of wonders was located. When they had reached the entrance, the castle guard whose duty it was to keep watch over the door came forth to greet the King.

The King told the guard to summon the keeper who presided over the chamber of wonders and to have him bring the wand of Hinun. The guard did as he was told.

The keeper arrived moments later. In his hand he held the wand of Hinun, a silver cloth wrapped around it so that the wand would not touch his hand. The King ordered him to give the wand to his son.

"Careful now. You must take the wand as I give it, and do not let it touch your hands bare," said the keeper, who was nervous about handing over the wand to the young prince. Sakima took the wand, praised his father for being such a man of his word, and off he went to test his knowledge in magic.

When the prince arrived at the double doors of his room, he pointed the wand at the doors and commanded them to open, but nothing happened. He tried again, but they remained closed So he went on ahead and opened the doors with his hands. Walking over to a shelf that was stationed near his bead, he withdrew a very old, heavily damaged book. Slowly, the prince turned to a page containing a spell for turning men into statues of stone.

Sakima pointed the wand at an apple on a tray in his room as he read the words on the page. "T'sah, T'sah, H'sah, Sa'vah!"

Again, nothing happened.

The prince then looked out his window and saw a squirrel climbing up a tree. He tried to cast a spell on the squirrel, but the squirrel just skittered away, unchanged.

Thinking there was something wrong with the wand, he turned it toward himself. Immediately the wand fired a blue beam of light, which struck him in the face. The prince was astonished. He got up and ran over to the mirror to see if anything had changed about his appearance, but all was normal.

"I cast my first spell," said the young prince. "I did it."

At that moment, there came a knock at his door. "Are you alright in there?" asked the Queen.

"Yes, all is well. I'm just moving some things around, Mother," Sakima said.

"Very well. Your father and I will be heading down to the garden for the live performance. Everyone is here to see you, son, so hurry on down," said the Queen, and she walked away.

"I'll be there," he yelled.

Placing the wand on his shelf, he walked over to his wardrobe. The prince pulled out the outfit that had been prepared for his birthday and quickly got dressed. But he was in such a hurry to get down to the garden that he did not notice that all who gazed upon him as he ran through the castle turned into statues of stone.

When the prince arrived outside, the people that saw him changed into statues of stone, but he did not notice any of it because he was in such a hurry. He heard the host call upon him to come up to the stage, so he rushed over.

"Everyone, I give you Prince Sakima," said the host. As soon as the prince walked onto the stage, the music stopped. He watched the host turn into a statue of stone right before his eyes. Puzzled by what he had just seen, Sakima walked over slowly to the host and felt his hands.

"Pure stone," said Sakima to himself.

Sakima turned to look for his parents. As soon as their eyes locked upon him, they turned to stone as well.

Sakima watched in horror as everyone who was present became statues before his eyes.

"What have I done?" asked the young prince. "I must have cursed myself."

He hopped down from the stage and ran over to his parents. Grabbing his mother by the hand, he said. "I'm going to fix this. I'm sorry."

Sakima placed his head on his mother's lap and wept. After spending a few minutes there by his parents' sides, he got up and ran back to his room. He grabbed the wand and the old book of spells from his bed. He searched for a counter spell—some way to undo what he had done—but the page with the reversal spell had been torn out of the old book.
Sakima searched through the book again and again, but he found nothing. He lay down on his bed and spent the rest of the evening there, mourning because there was nothing he could do to bring his parents back.

Many years passed by, and still Sakima searched for a way to undo the spell. But each time he hoped for an answer, it proved false. It seemed as though all hope was lost.

Then, one day ten years after he'd turned his parents to stone, a young lady named Everla came to visit her wealthy uncle in town. When she arrived at his home, the first thing she asked him about was the castle she had seen on her way to his home; it appeared to be abandoned.

Her uncle grabbed her bags and said, "Well, I can't tell you much about it. All we know is that half the town went to see the prince for his thirteenth birthday, and not a single one of them returned home. Many people have gone missing around here, too. You stay away from that place, Everla. It's dangerous."

"Okay," said Everla.

"I'll take your bags to the room," said her uncle.

Everla was a bit disturbed by her uncle's remarks, but she didn't make much of it.

"Will you be joining us for dinner, Everla?" her uncle asked as they walked toward the room where she would be sleeping during her stay.

"No, thank you, I'm fine. I think I'll take a walk out front. I've been sitting down for a long time. I need to move around," said Everla.

"Very well," said her uncle.

In the front yard, Everla saw a little girl running toward her, chasing her dog. The little girl called out to the dog, "Riffy, Riffy, come back here!"

"Do you need any help?" Everla yelled to the little girl.

"Yes, please!" said the little girl, who seemed to be out of breath. "You wait right there. I'll grab your dog," said Everla.

Everla took off on a wild chase behind the dog. Just before the gates to the castle, the dog finally stopped. Everla tried to creep up on her, but Riffy saw her coming. She wiggled herself through the bars of the gate and took off toward the castle.

Everla tried to open the gate, but it would not open, so she decided to look for another way in. As she was walking alongside the gate, she noticed some of the bars had been pried open. She squeezed through them and ran toward the castle, where she had last seen Riffy heading.

When she made it to the front of the castle, she called out to Riffy, but the dog did not respond. Suddenly a loud noise came from within the castle. Everla hurried toward the nearest window. She peeked inside, but she did not see anything. She tried the door. To her surprise, it opened.

Out of nowhere, Riffy ran into the castle. Everla tried to grab the dog, but she flew past her.

Riffy ran down a long hall, making a left at the corner. Everla followed, but when she went to turn left, she found a man in the middle of the hall with his bow drawn back. He was covered in armor.

Everla screamed.

"Stay where you are," said the man.

"I will," Everla said, surprised that there was someone in the castle. "What's your business here?" asked the man.
"I . . . I was just trying to retrieve a little girl's dog," Everla said. "She ran into the castle when I opened the door. I swear I . . . I thought this place was abandoned."

"What's your name?" asked the man. "Everla."

"You're not here to rob me?" he asked. "No," said Everla.

"And how do I know you're telling the truth?" he replied. "You don't," said Everla. "You're going to have to trust me."
While they were standing there talking, Riffy came and sat beside the man. He lowered his bow, picked up the dog, and handed her to Everla.

"Thank you kindly," said Everla, holding the dog in her arms.

The man turned and started to walk away. He was halfway down the hall when Everla shouted, "Wait!"

The man paused.

"Why are you wearing armor? It's hot outside," said Everla.

The man did not respond.

"Can I see the face of the man who helped me?" Everla asked, curious to see the face behind the helmet.

Do you wish to stay here forever?" asked the man.

"No," said Everla.

"Then I cannot show you my face." "Why?" asked Everla.
"Because I don't want you to see the monster that I have become. Please, shut the door on your way out."

And with that, the man walked away.

Everla stood still, watching as the man walked away. Turning, she saw the entrance to the Great Hall to her right. There was music playing, so she decided to take a look.

On the wall, she saw a huge painting of a king and his family. Everla was amazed at how much detail had been put into the painting.

Just then, Riffy started to bark at the painting. Everla tried to quiet her. A moment later, the man came and stood right beside her.

"You're still here," he said.

"Yes, I was just leaving. I'll be going now," Everla said, and she turned to walk away.

"It's okay. I love this painting, too. I couldn't have asked for better parents."
"Is that you?" asked Everla.
"Yes."

"I don't understand. What happened here?" Everla asked.
"If you truly wish to know, I'll tell you. It may take a bit of your time," said the prince.

"I have time," said Everla.

And so the prince told her his story, and when he was done, he stood with his hands behind his back as tears began to fall from his eyes, but of course, Everla could not see them because he had a helmet on.

"It's been a long time since I have looked up at this painting," said the prince.

"Beneath that mask is no monster," Everla said. "I've seen monsters before, and you're not one of them."

"Thank you, those were kind words," said the prince. Everla nodded. "I should be heading back."

The prince followed Everla to the door. As he held it open, she asked, "What is your name?"

"Sakima," the prince said.

"Sakima. I like that. It's . . . different," Everla said.

The two looked at each other for a moment. Then Everla said goodbye and set out to return the girl's dog.

Sakima watched her go. "She's beautiful," he said to himself.

The very next day, the prince began to clean up the castle. He did not know if Everla would come back, but if she did, he did not want it to look so abandoned.

As he picked up, he heard someone knocking at his front door. He peeked out the window and saw Everla below.

Sakima rushed down the stairs to meet her. When he got to the door, he paused and took a deep breath before opening it.

Everla bowed and then looked up at the prince.

Sakima was overtaken by her beauty. "I have not seen such beauty in all of the country," he said.

Everla smiled as she stood back up. In her hands was a book. She held it up before Sakima so he could read the title.

The Sacred Words," read the prince. "Interesting title."

"My uncle is a very wealthy man, and he spends much of his money and time collecting rare items. This book was amongst his collections. I sort of . . . borrowed it . . . from his library. It once belonged to a student of Hinun, named Koda."

"Koda," said the prince. He was amazed at what he was hearing.

"I figured we could search through it together," said Everla.

"Sure, sure, I'd love that," Sakima said.

Everla smiled.

"Come on in, I have something for you to see, too," said Sakima.

"Really, what is it?" asked Everla.

Sakima took her by the hand and led her to a room filled with statues.

"Who are these people?" asked Everla.

"Thieves whom fate delivered into the hands of the Stone Prince," said Sakima.

"There must be over a hundred statues in here," she said.

"Yes. There is a lot of treasure here, and since the castle appears to be abandoned, many think there is no one here to protect it. There have been many robbery attempts.

Unfortunately for them, I am here.

"My face is cursed," Sakima continued. "It's why I drew my bow at you. I thought you were one of them."

"So you turn them all into statues? Hmmm, serves them right," Everla said, rubbing her hand across the blade of a thief who had been turned into stone.

"If they ever wake, they will all be taken into custody. I've placed many of our guards around them, and chains around their legs, too," Sakima said. "There is one more thing I'd like to show you. I would like you to meet my family."

Everla nodded, but said nothing. Instead, she followed him out back to the garden, where thousands of statues stood facing the stage. Everla was amazed at the sight of it all.

"It's beautiful," she said.

Sakima told Everla the events that had transpired on that dreadful afternoon of his thirteenth birthday. "Not much has changed here," said Sakima. "It's like looking at a still picture. Everything is in the exact same place it was ten years ago. I've made sure it is kept neat and tended."

"Talk about time standing still," Everla said, looking about the garden. Sakima pulled some roses from the bushes by him and placed them on his mother's and father's laps.

"I miss them so much," he said, putting a hand on his mother's lap.

Everla took the book she was carrying with her and placed it on a table nearby. She grabbed Sakima by the hand and pulled him over. Together, the two spent the entire afternoon going through the writings of Koda.

Every day for three months straight, Everla showed up at the castle to read with Sakima. On the last day of the summer, when they were just about finished with the book, they found a spell that they both were sure could undo the spell of stone, but there was one problem. The spell could only be cast by the person who had cast the original spell, and Sakima was afraid of the wand of Hinun.

He had placed the wand in a secret place and vowed never to touch it again. Everla tried to talk him out of the vow, but nothing could persuade him. He was too afraid of its power.

Later on that evening, Everla and Sakima were enjoying a cup of tea together when they heard the sound of glass breaking downstairs. Sakima grabbed his bow. "Stay right here. I'll check it out," he said. But before he could get out of the room, someone jumped through the glass window where they were. Sakima struck him with his bow.

"We have to get you to safety!" said Sakima. "Where are we going?" asked Everla.

"Out the window," he said.

Everla grabbed the book, and they both snuck out the window. They climbed down the lattice, but when they got to the ground, they were seized by a band of robbers.

Sakima whispered to Everla to close her eyes, and she did. He removed his helmet, and all the robbers who stood about them were turned into statues of stone. Then, putting his helmet back on, he told Everla to run and hide in the garden.

She did not want to go without him, but Sakima told her that he had to go back. He needed to make sure the thieves didn't break any of the statues. "Be careful," said Everla.

She kissed him on his helmet and took off running toward the garden to hide. She didn't make it far before she was spotted by one of the thieves. He had seen her from the window on the second floor. The thief drew back his bow to strike Everla, but Sakima saw him. Sakima yelled at Everla to get down, but she could not make out his words; he was too far away. Everla turned around to face him at the same moment the thief released his arrow. Sakima pulled off his helmet, and for the first time, Everla saw his face. She smiled as she turned to stone.

Seconds later, the arrow struck her in the chest. But a mere arrow could not pierce the stone. It fell to the ground.

Frightened by what he had just seen, the thief tried to get away, but Sakima ran back into the castle to find him.

The thief tried to hide behind a column. Hearing Sakima enter the room, he fired a few arrows at him, but he kept missing. Sakima took off his helmet and tried to create a diversion by tossing it against the wall.

The intruder used the diversion as an opportunity to run over to a window where he could escape. He climbed up onto the window seal, but he did not jump. Instead, he tried once more to see if he could strike Sakima with his arrow. Placing an arrow onto his bow, he stood, waiting for Sakima to show his face. Sakima stepped out where the thief could see him. At once, the thief changed into stone. He fell from the window and shattered on the ground below.

Sakima went around to the back of the castle. Inside the dovecote was a ladder, which went up to a hidden room in the ceiling. Inside the room, Sakima walked toward a shelf with a brown chest on it.

Sakima pulled down the chest and withdrew the wand of Hinun inside. The wand was still covered in the silver cloth the keeper had wrapped it in ten years ago.

In spite of the gloves covering his hands, Sakima felt a surge of fear at the idea of touching the wand. Making sure only to touch the silver cloth, he picked up the wand.

A moment later, Sakima came out of the castle, the wand of Hinun in his hand. He walked over to Everla and took the book out of her hand.

"I wish there had been some other way to save you," he said. "It was the only way." And Sakima hugged the statue of Everla.

Placing the book on a nearby bush, he turned to the page that contained the spell that he and Everla had picked out. He pointed the wand at Everla and read the words off the page, but nothing happened. He tried again and again, and still, there was no magic. Sakima was sad. He could not understand why the spell would not work.

Sakima pulled his helmet off of his head and he slung it into the bushes. He gripped the wand so tightly in his frustration that he thought of breaking it, but the wand could sense that it was in danger and it released a blast of energy that knocked Sakima off of his feet, causing him to drop it on the ground.

Sakima jumped up and ran over to the wand to stomp on it, but the wand would not let his feet come upon it.

After a few more tries at destroying the wand, Sakima pulled off his gloves. He did not know what would happen if he touched the wand without the cloth, but as far as he was concerned, the worst things that could happen to him had already happened.

Bending down, Sakima picked up the wand. As soon as his hand touched it, the curse broke. He did not know that in order for the spell to be complete, he had to touch the wand with his bare hands. That part of the spell was not written down in the old book. But Sakima understood. The writings of Koda in Everla's book had explained his reasons for leaving certain things out of his spells.

Sakima stood there in a trance as he reflected on the things that he had read in the book that Everla had brought to him. He thought back to the day when he first asked his parents for the wand. He realized why his parents had not wanted to give him the wand—how they had tried to protect him from the wand. He watched as pieces of stone started to break off from the statues.

Soon, the air was filled with hundreds of thousands of pieces of stone flying in the air toward the wand. Sakima was shocked; he could not believe what he was witnessing.

The happiness he experienced at that moment seemed almost too much for him. He could barely hold on to the wand because of the shaking of his hands. The people whom he had caused to turn into stone were no longer statues anymore. They had returned unto their natural state, but they could not make sense of what had happened among them.

Sakima held on to the wand and watched as the pieces of stone that were left in the air were all drawn into the wand. When the last piece of stone disappeared, Sakima remembered Everla. Before he could turn around, he heard her move.

"I'm sorry I turned you into stone, Everla," Sakima said.

"You saved my life, Sakima," Everla said. "That arrow would have pierced my heart."

Sakima turned around slowly to face Everla. She stood still, a smile on her face.

Smiling back, Sakima ran over to her. He lifted her into the air and spun her around. Placing her back on the ground, he saw the crowd staring at the two of them in complete silence. They knew it was Sakima, but they couldn't believe it was him. He had grown up since the last time that they had seen him.

Sakima's parents stood up, and everyone grew quiet.

Slowly, Sakima walked over toward the king and queen. He fell to his knees, but his father came down and helped him up.

"Son, is it really you? You're all grown up," said the King. "I thought I'd never see the two of you again," said Sakima.

He tried to explain, but his father cut him off. He knew it was the wand all along. "Let it go, son. There is nothing you or I can do about the past," said the King.

Sakima nodded. "I want you to meet someone," he said and brought Everla over to his parents.

"She's beautiful," said the Queen.

Everla bowed, and that night the kingdom celebrated Prince Sakima's proposal to Everla.

The End

Enjoy Other Titles by Anboran

The Hairless Bear

The Candlemaker and the Moon

Changing Beautiful

Restoring Joy

Chandeliea

www.anboran.com

9 781732 536227